Дякую, thank you to my family and friends.

Published by A.Bamber | P.O. Box 22452 | San Francisco, CA 94122

This is a work of realistic fiction. Names, characters, businesses, places, events and incidents are either the products of the creator's imagination or used in a fictitious manner.

Publisher's Cataloging-In-Publication Data

Names: Bamber, Adrianna, author, illustrator.
Title: My Ukrainian American story / Adrianna Bamber.
Description: First edition. | [San Francisco, California] : [A.Bamber], 2017. | Interest age level: 003-007. |
Summary: "Oksana shares her rich Ukrainian American culture with you ... Experience the traditions, customs, dance, food, craft and music passed down from generations of Ukrainians. You'll be empowered to celebrate your own heritage after seeing how proud Oksana is of hers."--Provided by publisher.
Identifiers: LCCN 2017907035 | ISBN 978-0-9989591-0-8 (hardcover) | ISBN 978-0-9989591-1-5 (paperback)
Subjects: LCSH: Ukrainian Americans--Social life and customs--Juvenile fiction. | Ukraine--Social life and customs--Juvenile fiction. | CYAC: Ukrainian Americans--Social life and customs--Fiction. | Ukraine--Social life and customs--Fiction.
Classification: LCC PZ7.1.B36 My 2017 | DDC [E]--dc23

abamber.com

MyUkrainianAmericanStory.com

My
UKRAINIAN AMERICAN
Story

ADRIANNA BAMBER

Good day!
Say it with me in Ukrainian, Добрий день! (Do-bry den!)

My name is Oksana. I live in America with my parents who are from Ukraine. They taught me to speak Ukrainian and English; this means I am bilingual. I love my Ukrainian American culture and want to share it with you.

Let's start with the symbol on my shirt. It's a tryzub, the national emblem of Ukraine. Another symbol of Ukraine is this flag.

The blue stripe represents the sky and the yellow stripe represents a field of wheat.

So, where exactly is Ukraine?

Ukraine is in Eastern Europe. It is about 5,000 miles and seven time zones away from my home in New York.

When it is 2 pm for me, it is 9 pm at my cousin's home in Kyiv, the capital of Ukraine. I am almost done with my school day when my cousin is going to sleep.

On Saturdays, I go to Ukrainian school. I call it "Ukie School". It's where I'm taught about the geography, history and literature of Ukraine. Last week, I learned that Taras Shevchenko is the most celebrated Ukrainian poet and artist.

ІСТОРІЯ · HISTO
КУЛЬТУРА · CULTURE
ЧИТАНКА · RE
ГРАМАТИКА · GRAMMAR
ЛІТЕРАТУРА · LITERA
ГЕОГРАФІЯ · GEOGRAPHY
СЛОВНИК · DIC
УКРАЇНСЬКА МОВА · UKRAINIAN LANGUAGE

ЛЕСЯ УКРАЇНКА
(1871 – 1913)
Леся Українка писала про високі
ідеали і про нашу свободу.

НАДІЯ
Ні долі, ні волі у мене нема,
Зосталася тільки надія одна:

ЛЕСЯ УКРАЇНКА
1. Чому Українці читають
її твори?

2. Коли вона жила?

3. Про що вона писала?

This week, I am studying Ukraine's relationships with its neighbors.

I like reading and writing in Ukrainian. Some Ukrainian letters look exactly like English letters but they make different sounds.

I wrote the Ukrainian alphabet in my notebook for you. It has seven more letters than the English alphabet.

When my Ukrainian school classes are done, I take folk dance lessons. Some dances are only for girls or for boys and some dances are for both. Today we will dance the Hopak together; it's the national dance of Ukraine.

After many weeks of practice, we dance in front of an audience. I like these performances because we wear traditional outfits from Ukraine.

Not long ago, traditional clothing styles varied from region to region in Ukraine. These days, Ukrainian fashion styles are similar to American styles and traditional clothing is mostly worn for special events.

This is my favorite traditional Ukrainian outfit. My flower headpiece is called a vinok and my coral beads are called korali.

Traditional Ukrainian music is also played for special events. My bandura plays like a guitar but sounds like a harp. The tsymbaly is played with mallets and sounds similar to a harpsichord.

The trembita is played in the Carpathian Mountains in Ukraine. It sounds a bit like a bugle horn. My grandfather, who I call Dido, knows how to play it.

When I stay with Dido in Ukraine, we visit wooden churches. These churches smell and look like the ones in the New York mountains.

Most of the Ukrainian churches I have seen in Ukrainian and American cities have gold domes. Inside are colorful stained glass windows, icons and embroidered fabrics.

Embroidery has a long and important history in Ukraine. My grandmother, who I call Baba, teaches me about the symbolism of the colors and designs.

My first embroidery project is a small pillow. This challenging project seems to take forever, just like the wait for summer.

I love summer because I go to Ukrainian scout camp. Here, I see friends I haven't seen since last summer plus I make new friends. Together we learn about nature and earn patches for our uniforms.

At night, we tell stories, perform skits and sing songs by a big crackling bonfire.

At the end of summer, my family vacations at a Ukrainian resort in the Catskill Mountains in New York. All of the buildings are named after villages or cities in Ukraine.

A few of my camp friends and their families vacation here at the same time. We hike, swim and eat Ukrainian food together.

Ukrainian food is very tasty, especially when I help make it. My mom and I make Baba's recipe for potato dumplings called pyrohy or varenyky.

We also make beet soup called borsch and stuffed cabbage rolls called holubtsi. Traditionally, this food is for family gatherings and holiday celebrations. My favorite holiday is...

Saint Nicholas Day. During the Christmas play at my Ukrainian school, Saint Nicholas, called Sviati Mykolai, gives gifts to well behaved children.

On Christmas Eve, my family celebrates traditions from Ukraine. At the sight of the first star in the sky, we begin a twelve-course meal called Sviata Vechera. After this delicious meal is finished, we attend mass at church.

Another holiday I like to celebrate is Easter. Before Easter, I make pretty eggs called pysanky. Similar to embroidery, all the colors and designs have special meanings from long ago.

When I am finished with my pysanky, they will decorate a basket filled with symbolic food. This food will be blessed then enjoyed on Easter Sunday.

Yikes! I have to go now but it was fun to share my Ukrainian American story with you. I am off to meet my family at my favorite restaurant in the Ukrainian Village in New York City.

Goodbye! До побачення! (Do po-ba-chen-nya!)

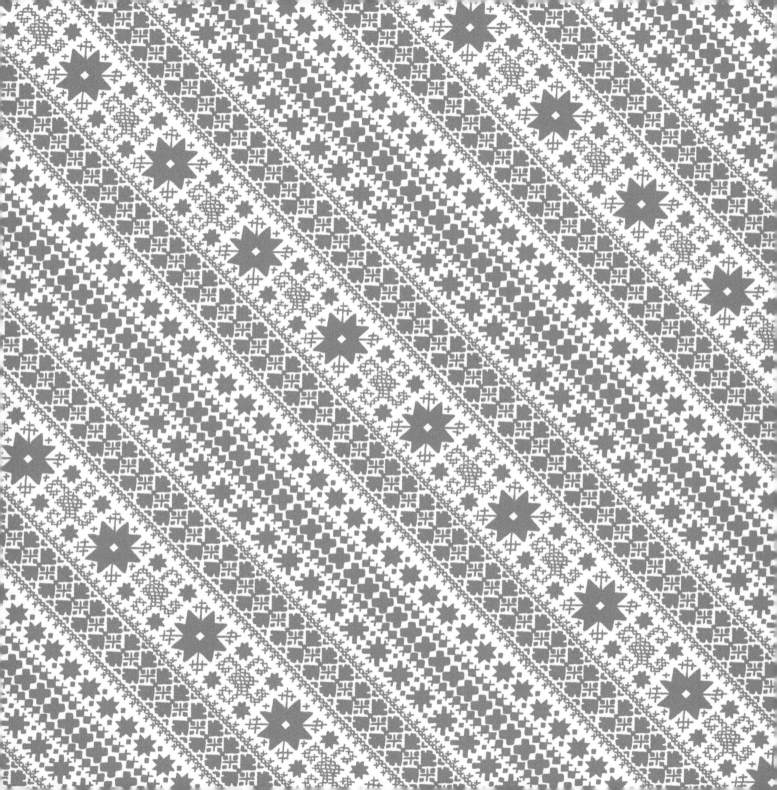

ADRIANNA OKSANA BAMBER is a Ukrainian American author and illustrator. As a child she was often told that she would grow up to appreciate her culture. As it turns out, this is true.

"My Ukrainian American Story" is her first picture book. She lives in beautiful San Francisco, California.

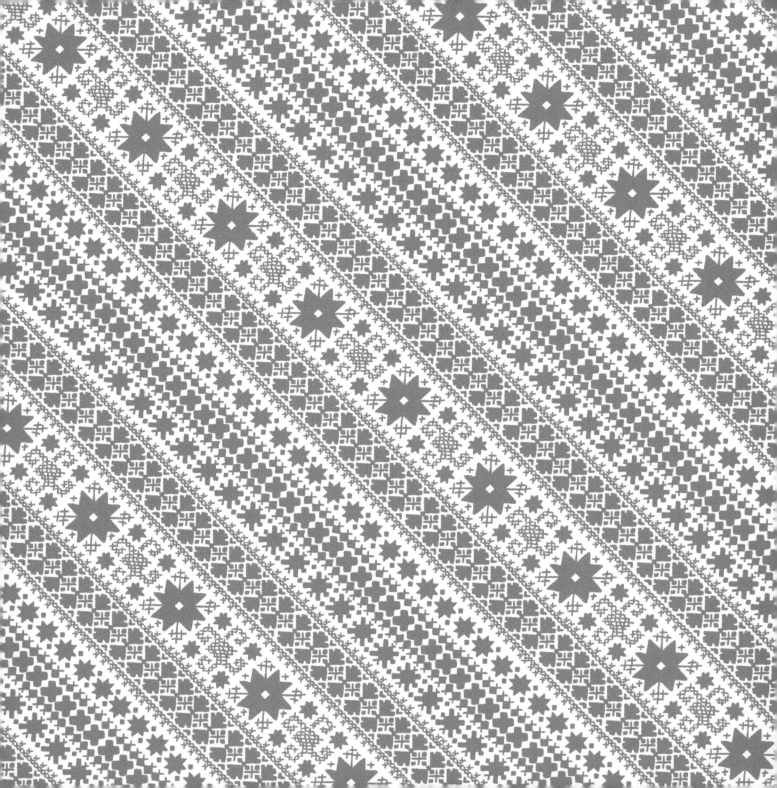

CPSIA information can be obtained
at www.ICGtesting.com
Printed in the USA
LVHW071815100322
713133LV00007B/377